For Ari and Milo and all those who have tried
so hard to make me happy. —E.T.B.

Thank you, Jet, for teaching me how to draw. —J.M.

 Hippo Park

An imprint of Astra Books for Young Readers, a division of Astra Publishing House
astrapublishinghouse.com
Printed in China

ISBN: 978-1-6626-4004-9 (hc)
ISBN: 978-1-6626-4005-6 (eBook)
Library of Congress Control Number: 2021922640

First edition

10 9 8 7 6 5 4 3 2 1

Design by Amelia Mack
The text is set in Wonder.
The illustrations are done digitally.

HOW TO DRAW

A HAPPY CAT

Story by
**Ethan T.
Berlin**

Drawn by
**Jimbo
Matison**

Hippo Park

Learning how to draw a **happy** cat is fun and easy!

First, draw two rounded rectangles.

Next, draw two triangles for ears and two big dots for

Then, add a triangle for a nose
lines for stripes and whiskers.

Now, draw legs and a tail.
Add some color!

Finally, add a mouth.

**Hmm, she doesn't look very happy.
What do you think she wants?**

Let's give her a cool T-shirt.

And a stuffy?

Oh, I know—a skateboard!

Great. She's totally **happy** now!

And now . . .

She's not.

Let's draw her some friends!

And a **ramp!**

Great! She's so **happy!**

Good job!

Uh-oh!

What's the problem, Cat?

Oh, she's scared of landing from this high up.

Quick! Draw an airplane!

Great! Now she's a **happy** cat!

That didn't last very long!
What's going on this time, Cat?

Right, all this skateboarding with friends
on top of an airplane has made her hungry.

Let's see . . .

Draw a pizzeria!

But, Cat, how are you going to get the pizza?

Um, you want us to draw a giant pizza catapult?

Listen, Cat, we're trying hard to make you happy here, but catapulting pizza at you while you're skateboarding on top of an airplane sounds like

a real bad idea.

okay,
okay!

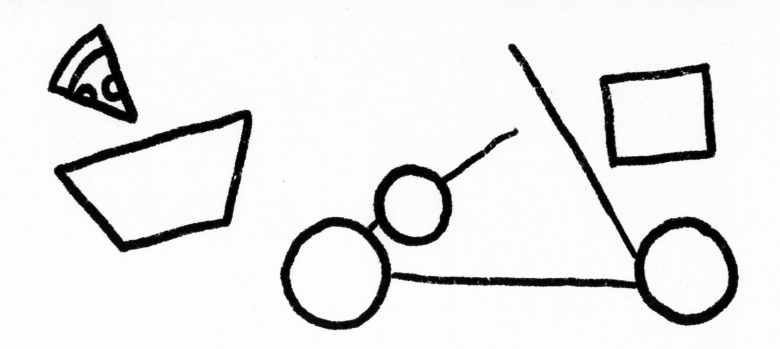

Draw some circles and a big triangle and a scoopy thing.

Here's your pizza catapult, Cat.

Yummm!

Uh-oh! Some of the pizza got in the plane's engine. Who could have seen **that** coming?

Quick, draw parachutes!

And parachutes for the pizza.

Phew! Everyone is safe on the ground and their bellies are full.

Cat wants to **celebrate!**

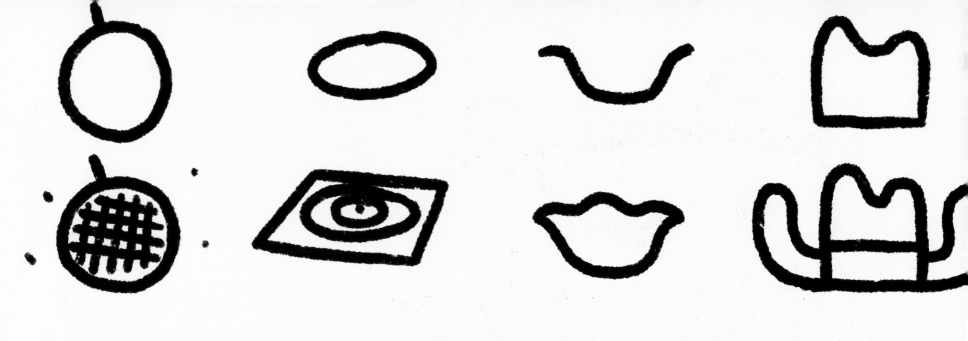

Draw the **most awesome party ever,**
with really cool hats, ice cream sundaes, a DJ, a disco ball . . .

And a dolphin riding a scooter!

And that's how you draw a **happy** cat!

But now Chicken is sad.